Wind

Dedicated to my
grandchildren

Lois Pressler

Dedicated to
my buddy, Isaiah

Joy Troyer

Published by Double Ray Press, 2007
Terra Ceia, Florida
In cooperation with Dyeing Arts
www.dyeingarts.com

Printed in the U.S. by Lightning Source, Inc.
www.lightningsource.com

ISBN 0-9761206-1-5

Book designed by Joy Troyer

Wind

By Lois Irene Mann Pressler

Illustrated by Joy Troyer

I'll tell you a secret
I've got a friend
He's bold and outrageous
His name is Wind.

Sometimes
when he whispers
so soft in the trees
I call him his nickname,
"Summertime Breeze."

I lie in my bed
at the end of the day
And listen real careful
to what he will say.

Sometimes he is quiet

not there at all.

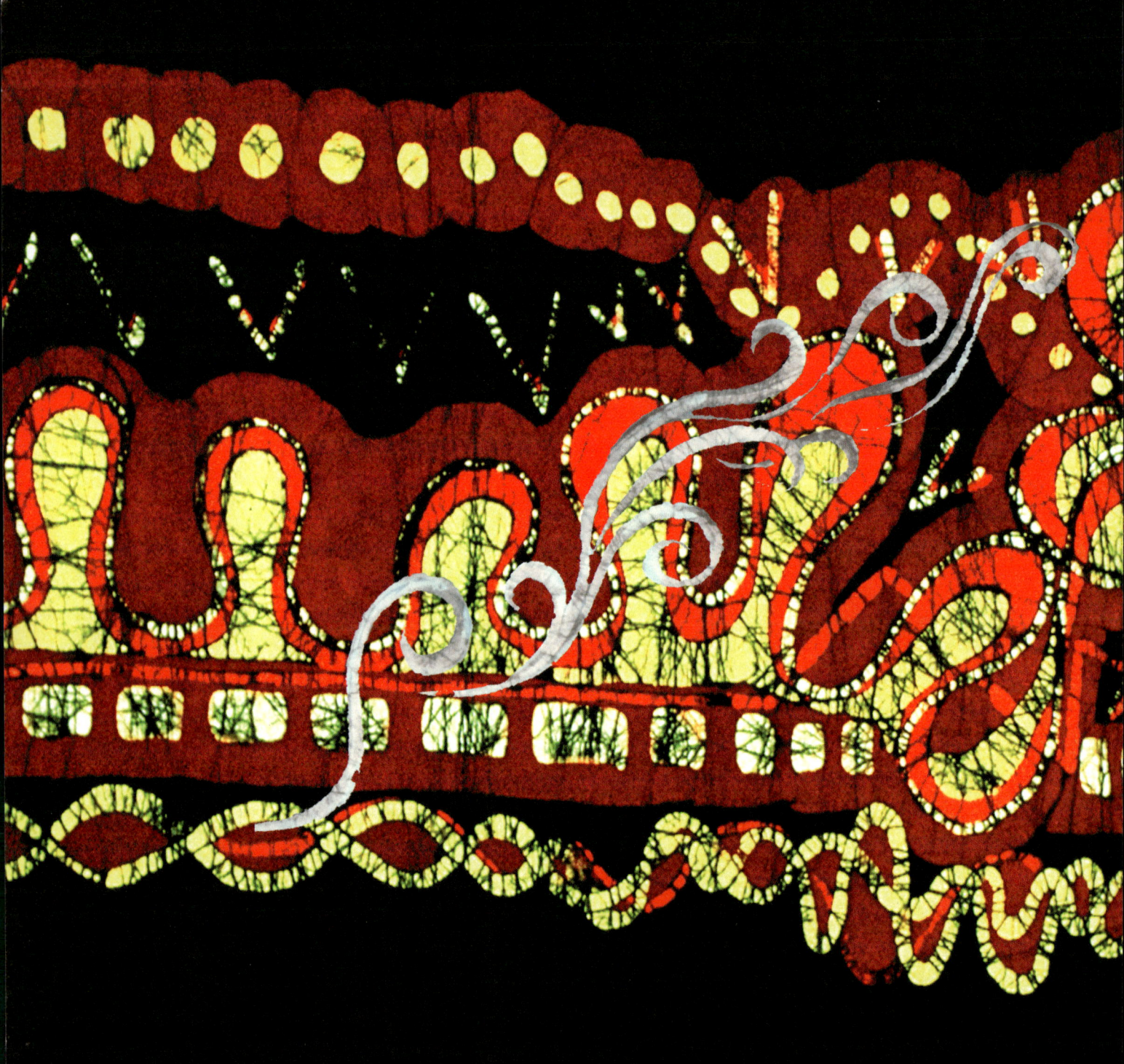

Sometimes I can hear him

clear out in the hall.

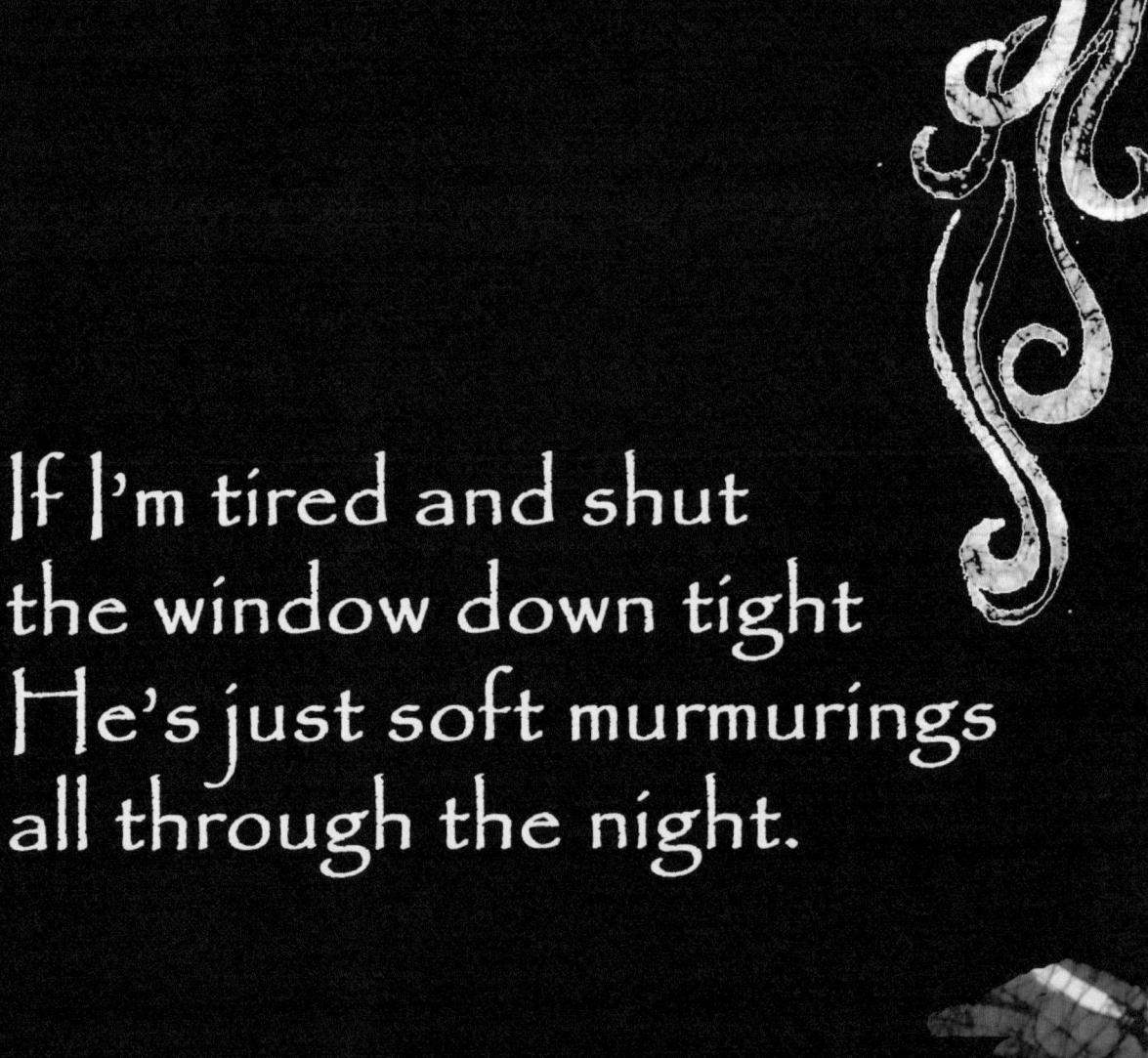

If I'm tired and shut
the window down tight
He's just soft murmurings
all through the night.

What's really the best
is the window flung wide
Then he's all
rattles and riffles inside.

He talks of lands
he's traveled afar

Java and
Uzbek
and bright
Zanzibar.

He carries the flick
of the steamy heat

and he moans the pulse
of the jungle beat.

I hear lions
and tigers
when I close
my eyes,
and bongo drums
and baboon cries.

He speaks the language
of lands he's seen.

Rivers ...

and oceans ...

and
forests
green

I feel the world ...

and
hear
its
sound.

I have great fun
when Wind's around.

Lois Irene Mann Pressler

is the mother of three grown children, grandmother of seven, and has loved and nurtured countless others. Pressler, born in 1919, began writing during high school. During her years of work, first as a chemist and then as a church and community volunteer, she never lost her interest in words. At the age of 79 she co-authored a novel, *First Woman*, with her daughter, Terra. At 82 she began writing stories and poetry for her grandchildren.

Elephant

I have a pet elephant in our big garage.
Mother doesn't want him roaming at large.
Neighbors might think him vicious or mean.
We're sorry -- he did punch a hole in their screen.

We call our back yard a big circus tent
And Elephant and I play at games we invent.
Elephant makes all the animals mind.
He's really quite seriously gentle and kind.

We've taught my stick horse to preen and to prance.
Good old Brown Bear is learning to dance.
Pigtail rag doll flies high in the swing
And my monkey, Rolf, does tricks on the ring.

When circus is over, we like to play school.
Elephant then climbs up on the stool.
He teaches us history, some Latin and art.
We think that coloring's the very best part.

I like to serve late afternoon tea;
Just Grandma and Grandpa, Elephant and me.
Elephant likes his a little bit sweet
And he's always polite and most carefully neat.

Grandma and I always have a good talk
About beetles and bugs and why fish cannot walk.
Elephant and I are learning a lot.
Some of it's nice and some of it's not.

Elephant is really my very best friend.
When night time has come and the day's at an end
And I am so sleepy I can't sit up right,
Grandpa tucks both of us in for the night.

Lois Irene Mann Pressler

Joy Troyer, artist, learned batik from a book just before turning 40. Later she took studio art workshops at Esalen Institute in Big Sur, California and at the University of Minnesota's Split Rock Arts program. Courses at United Theological Seminary of the Twin Cities helped Joy find direction for her artwork. She creates large wall art using themes of nature and spirituality. All the illustrations in this book are batik or fabric paintings. Joy also used batik to illustrate *The Everything Seed* children's picture book and Dyeing Arts cards.

Also illustrated by Joy Troyer

The Everything Seed
A Story of Beginnings
by Carole Martignacco
Published by Tricycle Press

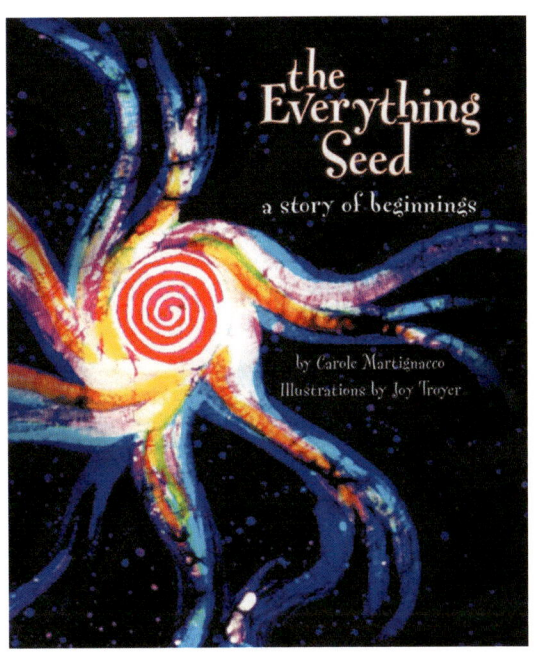

PowerPoint presentations in English, Spanish, and French.
Resource Guide for classes and worship
Greeting cards
www.DyeingArts.com

ISBN: 13:978-1-58246-161-8
ISBN: 10:1-58246-161-9

Acknowledgements

Thanks to Carolyn Pressler & Terra Pressler
whose love of and belief in their mother
made this book possible.

Thanks to Michael Peterson
who provided encouragement to Joy
throughout the publishing process.

Thanks to Paul Pressler,
Lois' husband, for his unstinting support.

Printed in the United States
152227LV00002B